D1243439
FLORENCE
BLUE MOSQUE
ISTANBUL - TURKEY
WELCOME TO
NEW YORK CITY
WELCOME TO
FCB
ישראל
SAINT PETERSBURG
RUSSIA
BRAZIL
BRAZIL
Rio de Janeira
HAWAII
Aloha
HAWAII
BERLIN
BRANDENBURG GATE
GERMANY
VENICE
VENICE
ROMA
ITALY
DESTINATIONS
DUBLIN
CHINA BEIJING CHINA
Beijing
CANADA VANCOUVER CANADA
Vancouver
EDINBURGH
Scotland
UK
EDINBURGH

BLUE MOSQUE
ISTANBUL - TURKEY
WELCOME TO
NEW YORK CITY
WELCOME TO
Cairo
FCB
ישראל
Rio de Janeiro
HAWAII
Aloha
HAWAII
SAINT PETERSBURG
BERLIN
BRANDENBURG GATE
GERMANY
VENICE
VENICE
ROMA
ITALY
DESTINATIONS
DUBLIN
VANCOUVER CANADA
Vancouver
CHINA BEIJING CHINA
Beijing
EDINBURGH
UK
Scotland

This Book Belongs To

The Adventures of

Bella & Harry

Let's Visit Florence!

Written by

Lisa Manzione

Illustrated by

Kristine Lucco

Bella & Harry, LLC

"Bella,
please sit still!"

"Oh, Harry. . . I am trying to sit still! How much longer is it going to take you to finish my portrait?"
"Bella, don't rush me! I am a master at work. . . just like Leonardo da Vinci!"

"Ha! Ha! Harry,
what do you know about
Leonardo da Vinci?"

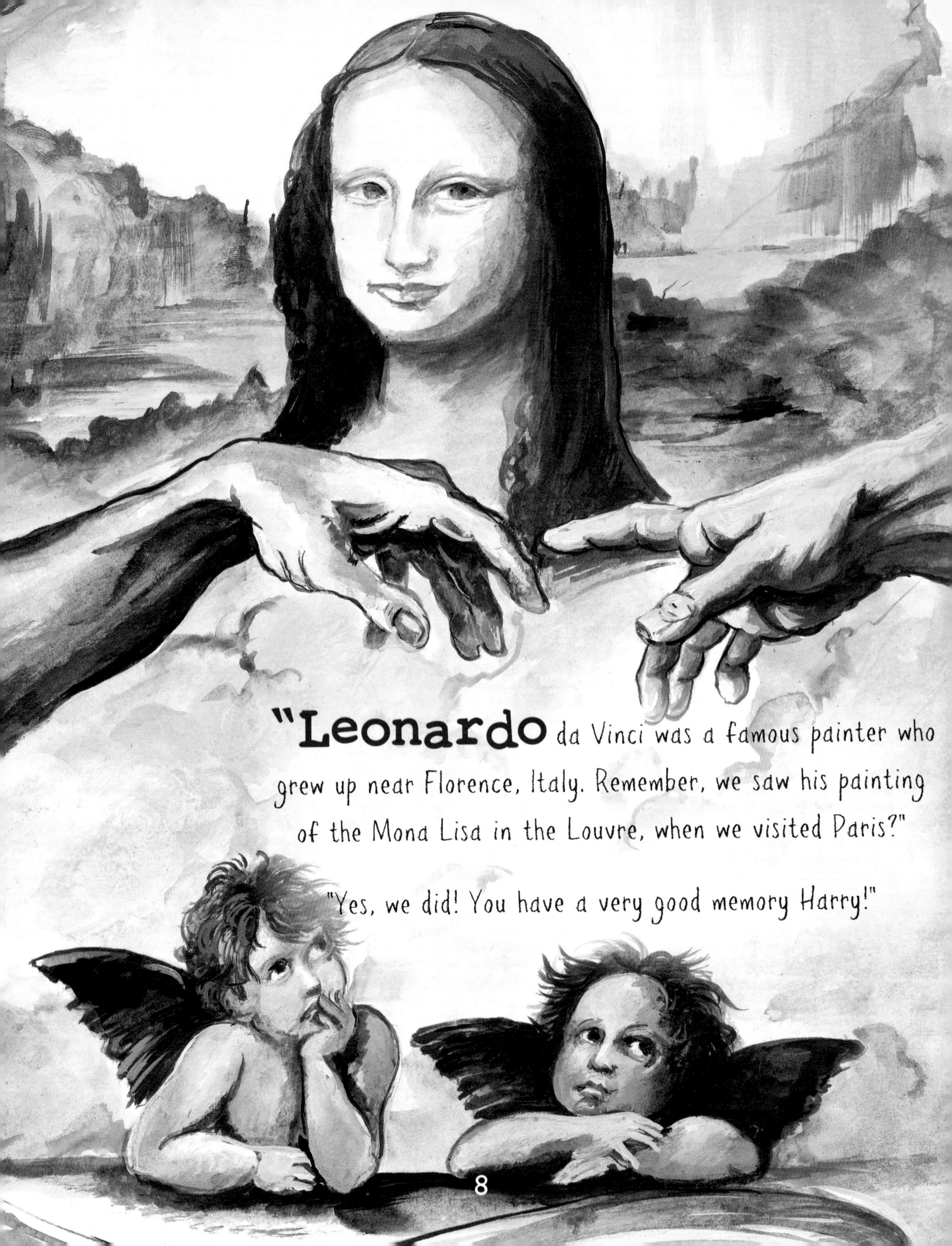

"**Leonardo** da Vinci was a famous painter who grew up near Florence, Italy. Remember, we saw his painting of the Mona Lisa in the Louvre, when we visited Paris?"

"Yes, we did! You have a very good memory Harry!"

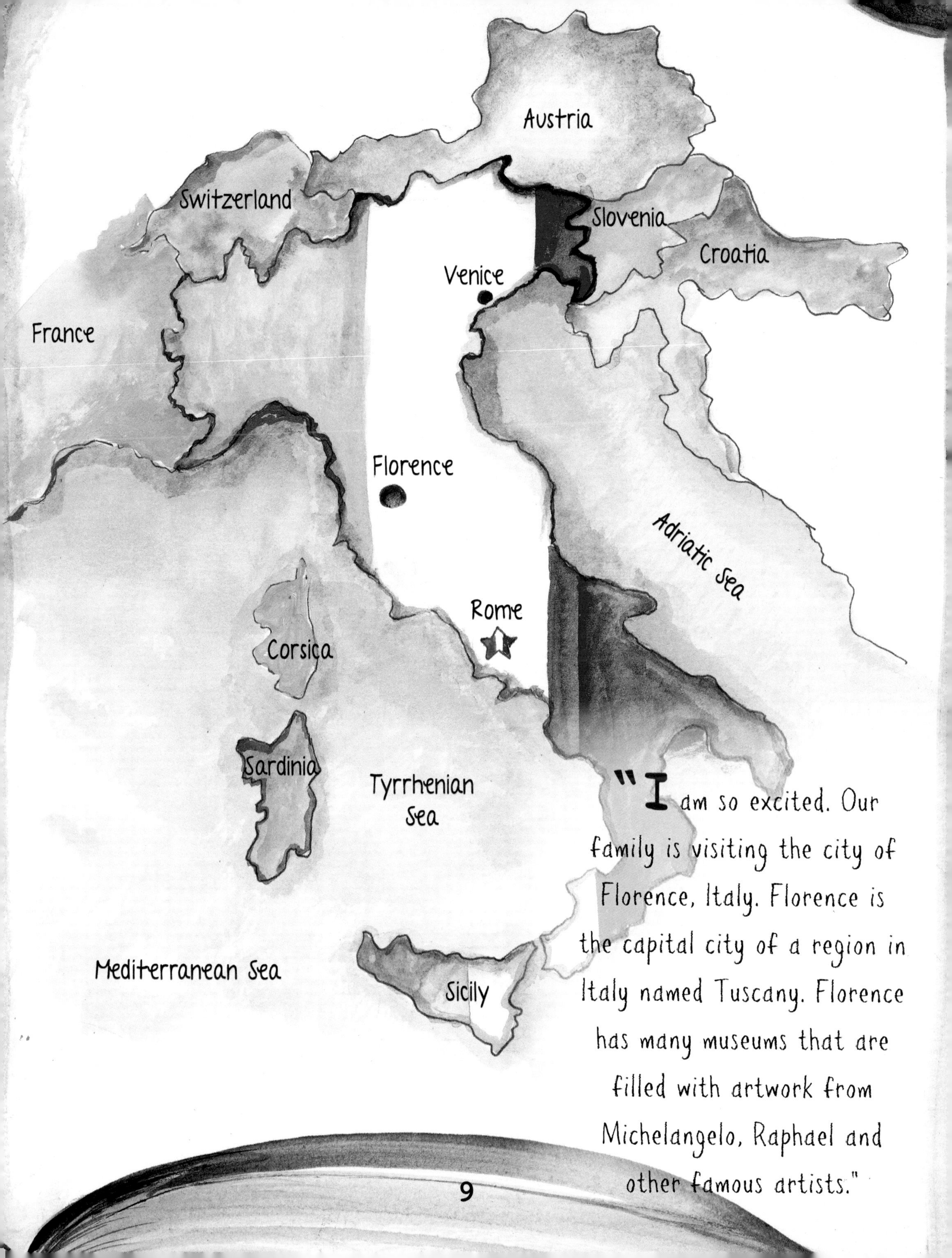

"I am so excited. Our family is visiting the city of Florence, Italy. Florence is the capital city of a region in Italy named Tuscany. Florence has many museums that are filled with artwork from Michelangelo, Raphael and other famous artists."

HARRY
"Perfect, Harry! I love my
portrait! Let's race to the Uffizi Gallery
and compare your artwork to the Masters!"

"Do you have the tickets, Bella?"

"Yes, I do."

"Bella, I like saying Uffizi Gallery!
It sounds like 'u-feet-zee'! Ha! Ha!"

Bella and Harry roamed the halls of the Uffizi Gallery looking at works of art from famous artists such as Caravaggio, Botticelli, Rembrandt and da Vinci.

All the paintings were so colorful! Both Bella and Harry loved spending time in the gallery.

"**That** was a lot of fun! Now we are off to the 'Piazza del Duomo'! Don't you just love Italian words, Harry? They just roll right off your puppy tongue! Piazza! Piazza! Piazza!"

"Yeah! I love pizza!!!"

"**Ha! Ha!** Funny, Harry! No, we are not going to have pizza. We are going to a piazza, a place where people meet. The Piazza del Duomo is in the middle of Florence and it is where the 'Florence Baptistery' is located. The Piazza del Duomo is also known as Cathedral Square."

"**Bella,** what is the Florence Baptistery?"

"The Florence Baptistery, also known as the Baptistery of Saint John, is one of three religious buildings that are part of the Piazza del Duomo complex. The Baptistery has three sets of doors that are made of bronze. The doors were designed by two famous artists, Andrea Pisano and Lorenzo Ghiberti. Each square on the doors shows a different religious scene."

"Wow! Bella, these doors are very beautiful!"

"They sure are, Harry. Let's take a closer look at them."

The Baptistery is shaped like an octagon, which means it has eight sides.

"**The** second building is the 'Florence Cathedral', or Cathedrale di Santa Maria del Fiore (Cathedral of Saint Mary of the Flowers). This is the main church in Florence. The dome of the cathedral is made of brick and to this day, remains the largest brick dome ever made. Many people also call this church il Duomo or il Duomo di Firenze."

"**The** third building of the complex is 'Giotto's Campanile Tower'. This thin tower is 277.9 feet tall and there are 7 bells in the tower."

"**Next** stop. . . the Arno River! We are going to board a 'barchetto' (an old style gondola boat) and cruise the river. The river starts way up in Monte Falterona and flows through Florence, all the way to the Tyrrhenian Sea."

"Smile,
Harry. Our family is taking our picture in front of the Arno River as it passes through Florence."

"**Hey,** Bella, remember when we were in Venice and you fell out of the gondola? You were so busy telling me to be careful; YOU fell out of the gondola instead of me! That was VERY funny!"

"Yes, Harry. I remember, but I was only a puppy when I fell out of the gondola. That will not happen again!"

While Bella was busy telling Harry about the bridge, she made a quick turn in the gondola and lost her balance. Bella fell right out of the gondola and into the Arno River! Luckily, Harry was there to help her out of the water.

Now that Bella was dry from her dip in the Arno River, she and Harry were off to the Galleria dell'Accademia to see "David" by Michelangelo. This famous statue has been kept at the museum since 1873.

"HOW tall is
this statue, Bella?"

"This statue is 17 feet tall
and is made of marble."

"Bella, did you notice he
doesn't have any clothes on?
HEE! HEE!"

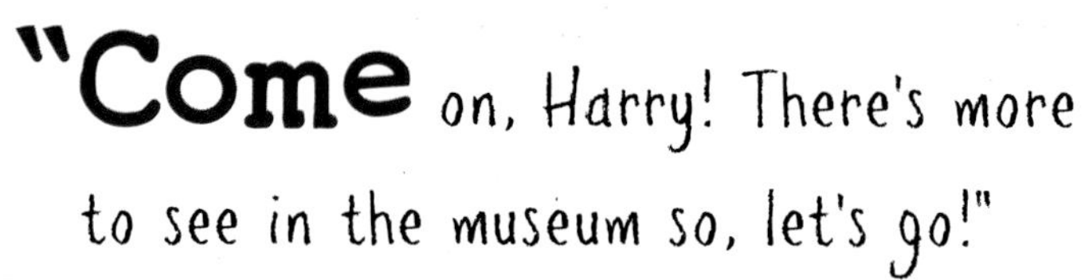

"Come on, Harry! There's more to see in the museum so, let's go!"

"**Oh,** Bella, a street artist. Let's have him draw a picture of us."

"Smile, Harry!!!"

"**Bella**, on our way back to the hotel, let's stop and try to find the perfect hat as a souvenir of our trip."

We had a great time in Florence, but it's time to explore the rest of Tuscany. We hope you will join us on our next adventure. For now it's good-bye, or "arrivederci" in Italian, from Bella Boo and Harry too!

Our Adventures in Florence

Bella visiting one of the jewelry stores on the Ponte Vecchio (also known as the Gold Bridge).

Bella and Harry enjoying a typical Tuscan meal of pappa al pomodoro (tomato and bread soup), panzanella (salad made with bread and tomatoes) and bistecca alla Florentina (Florentine steak).

Harry took a side trip to the town of Pisa and visited the famous Leaning Tower of Pisa.

Bella and Harry stopped to see il Porcellino, the famous bronze boar fountain. Legend says, if you rub the nose of the boar, it means you will come back to Florence again for a visit.

Fun Italian Words and Phrases

I don't understand. - Non capisco.

Do you speak English? -
Parli inglese?

How are you? - Come stai?

Thank you very much. - Grazie mille.

What's your name? -
Come ti chiama?

I'm hungry. - Ho fame.

I'm tired. - Sono stanco.

Library of Congress Cataloging-in-Publications Data is available

Manzione, Lisa

The Adventures of Bella & Harry: Let's Visit Florence!

ISBN 978-1-937616-59-5

First Edition

Book Nineteen of Bella & Harry Series

For further information please visit:

BellaAndHarry.com

or

Email: BellaAndHarryGo@aol.com

Printed in the United States of America

Phoenix Color, Hagerstown, Maryland

March 2017

17 3 19 PC 1 1

BLUE MOSQUE
ISTANBUL - TURKEY
WELCOME TO
NEW YORK CITY
WELCOME TO
Cairo
FCB
SAINT PETERSBURG
BERLIN
BRANDENBURG GATE
GERMANY
HAWAII
Aloha
HAWAII
BRAZIL
Rio de Janeiro
ROMA
ITALY
VENICE
DESTINATIONS
DUBLIN
VANCOUVER CANADA
Vancouver
CHINA BEIJING CHINA
Beijing
EDINBURGH
UK
EDINBURGH
Scotland

Cairo
SAINT PETERSBURG
RUSSIA
DESTINATIONS
VANCOUVER CANADA
CANADA VANCOUVER
Vancouver
ROMA
FCB
BERLIN
BRANDENBURG GATE
GERMANY
EDINBURGH
EDINBURGH
Scotland
UK
EDINBURGH
NEW YORK CITY
WELCOME TO
RIO DE JANEIRO
BRAZIL
Rio de Janeiro
ישראל
CHINA BEIJING CHINA
Beijing
HAWAII
Aloha
BLUE MOSQUE
ISTANBUL - TURKEY
FLORENCE